Rachel's Roses

written by Karen Christensen
illustrated by Bernadette Watts

BAREFOOT BOOKS
BATH

Grandma came to visit. Her arms were full
of flowers from her garden. They were for
Rachel's Mummy. In her straw shopping
basket was a small bundle, wrapped in
newspaper and tied with string. These flowers
were for Rachel. They were ROSES.

Rachel pressed her nose against the roses.
The pink rosebuds had a sweet, cool smell.
They were tight and smooth.

Mummy showed Rachel how to cut the dry ends of the stems before putting the flowers into fresh water. They put the rosebuds into a fine vase.

Every morning, Rachel checked the water in her vase of roses. Roses are thirsty on warm summer days. Sometimes they need an extra drink.

The roses began to open. Rachel could see their yellow hearts. The smell was deep and strong and glad. Sometimes a bee came to drink their sweetness.

One morning, Rachel saw that the roses were hanging their heads. Their petals were beginning to fall off. She gave them extra water, but the roses did not change. She bent her head low, breathing in their scent.

When she went to see the roses the next
morning, the vase was gone. Mummy had put
the roses in the bin! 'They're not dead – they're
not!' Rachel shouted.

Mummy tried to explain, but Rachel sat on
the floor with the roses in her lap. She cried. At
last Mummy went to the telephone. She called
Grandma and told her what had happened.
As they talked and Rachel watched, Mummy
began to write on a piece of paper.

They laid Rachel's roses on the windowsill,
and at the weekend they went to a nursery
with the note Mummy had written.

Mummy helped Rachel choose a small woody plant in a pot of dark earth speckled with white stones. It had a plastic tag on it with a picture of pink roses.

Rachel and Mummy dug a hole under
Rachel's bedroom window for the new rose
bush. They laid the old, dry roses on the earth
under the new rose bush, along with some
straw from the rabbit hutch.

When autumn came, they put tea leaves and
some wilted carrots and potato peelings
around the rose plant, and dug them well in.

Christmas came and it began to snow. How cold and white the garden was! The rose bush was almost bare, with only a few brown leaves clinging to its stems. Mummy said it was resting, waiting for spring to come.

One day there were crocuses and primroses in the border, and daffodils across the lawn.

Rachel went out in her boots and peered at the stems of her rose bush. Tiny ruffled shoots were pushing out from the bumps on the stem.

Then the swallows returned.

Thrushes tapped the ground for worms.
The shoots on the bush grew bigger and
longer. New, reddish leaves fluttered and
turned green.

One day Rachel put on a straw hat and spread
a rug beside her rose bush. There were some
tight green buds, reaching for the sky.

'I'm waiting for the roses,' Rachel said, but
the roses didn't come and she had to go
inside for tea.

At last the buds grew fat enough to burst. The spring winds dropped. The sun shone and it was June again. And there one morning under her window, nodding their heads 'hello', were Rachel's roses.

How to grow your own Rose Bush

Roses come in many colours: pink, red, white, yellow, even peach and lavender! But you may not see flowers on the plant when you buy it. The best time of the year to plant roses is in the autumn, when the flower stems have been cut back, or pruned, to help the rose grow strong again during the winter.

Some rose bushes are sold in pots of soil, others are bare-root plants. Whichever you buy, be sure to keep the roots moist before and after you put the plant in the ground.

The bud union is the place from which the rose stock grows upwards and the roots grow downwards. In warm climates, and in sheltered gardens, you should let the bud union show just above the surface of the soil, so that the sun can reach it. In cold climates, place the bud union an inch or two below the surface to protect it from winter cold. Give your plant plenty of room (at least twelve inches) all around. Roses like fresh breezes and are less likely to get mildew on their leaves when the air can blow around them.

During the autumn, feed your rose bush with natural fertilizers such as manure, fish emulsion and compost. A mulch of well-rotted manure is a good idea because it makes the soil soft and rich. Roses also like a handful of bone meal in the spring.

Barefoot Beginners
an imprint of
Barefoot Books Ltd
PO Box 95
Kingswood
Bristol BS30 5BH

Cover design by Jennifer Hoare
Printed in Singapore by Tien Wah Press Pte Ltd
ISBN: 1 901223 57 4
3 5 7 9 8 6 4 2

BAREFOOT BOOKS publishes high-quality picture books for
children of all ages and specialises in the work of artists and writers from
many cultures. If you have enjoyed this book and would like to receive a copy of
our current catalogue, please contact our London office – tel: 0171 704 6492
fax: 0171 359 5798 email: sales@barefoot-books.com
website: www.barefoot-books.com